# Calamity Rayne Over the Moon

## A NOVELLA

### CALAMITY RAYNE
### BOOK FOUR

## LYDIA MICHAELS

Calamity Rayne Over the Moon
The Calamity Rayne Series
©2024 by Lydia Michaels Books
Romantic Comedy
BAILEY BROWN PUBLISHING

# READING ORDER

Calamity Rayne Gets a Life (1)

Calamity Rayne Back Again (2)

Calamity Rayne Gets Hitched (3)

Calamity Rayne Veiled & Railed (3.5)

Calamity Rayne Over The Moon (4)

Visit www.LydiaMichaelsBooks.com for your FREE eBook of Calamity Rayne Veiled & Railed

# Dedication

*For Mimi*
*Thanks for all the giggles! Never lose that*
*sizzle!*
*Your friend,*
*Lydia*

*Listen to the Calamity Rayne Playlist!*
Click Here to Listen!

# Failure to Launch

I'VE NEVER MADE IT A SECRET THAT I struggle with the adulting. I mean, one year ago my life looked completely different. I was paying off loads of college debt, not using my degree, and blissfully living paycheck to paycheck while bartending at an underwhelming hole in the wall in Oregon. So how did I get here? Well, it's an interesting story—and a hot one—with a lot of unpredictable twists and jaw-dropping turns.

Honestly, I've barely had time to catch my breath since I shifted from the pokey lane to the jet-set lifestyle of a billionaire's wife. Yep, I said billionaire—with a big old B. He's not a dick either. But he does have a big one.

To be clear, it's never been about the money for me. It was a little about the personal chef he had when we met because food is my porn. And a lot about the orgasms, because I never knew such things were possible for me. But never about his fortune.

No clue how I landed my own personal Prince Charming. It's not like I came with any sort of sex skills or strategy. But somehow, in all of my clumsy awkwardness, Hale fell in love with the real me.

*That's Hale sleeping right over there...*

Sure, he doesn't look like much in that chin-to-chest dad-pose with his hands folded around that plush unicorn but, believe me, when he's conscious and vertical he's a total smoke show.

He's resting because we have a ten-month-old daughter who just started walking. Chasing her little butt around is freaking exhausting.

*That's Peanut sleeping next to him...*

Sure, she looks all innocent now, curled up like a little cherub with her Meep Meep sheep, but I promise there are little nubs under those soft curls where horns are starting to grow. She's only in the button-buck stages of demonized behavior, so I'm still hopeful. But if her tongue starts to fork, we're in trouble.

I sighed. Who was I kidding? They were both perfect.

Yes, Hale was a bit of a neatnik operating under some severe and technically undiagnosed OCD. But those control freak proclivities had served him well so far.

And Elara—a.k.a. Peanut—well, she was the other love of my life and just as stubborn as her father. Yes, the Davenport DNA was strong in that one. I was going to miss her while we were gone.

Chewing my lip, I glanced at the various stacks of new clothes. How was I ever going to fit all of that into those tiny suitcases?

It had been one week since the wedding, and the guests—aside from Hale's mom and the nanny—were all gone. Thank God.

Don't get me wrong, I appreciated everyone coming out to celebrate with us, but people were exhausting. And 99.9% of those guests were Hale's friends, not mine.

I had eleven guests at our wedding. Eleven. Hale had three-hundred and twelve.

Suffice it to say, I was ready to get away. It had been weeks since I'd been home and our flight was leaving in twelve hours.

My stomach hurt every time I considered how long we would actually be gone and how much Elara would change. Two months seemed excessive, but billionaires liked to be extra.

I glanced back at the two of them. The fading sun illuminated the Manhattan skyline, casting Hale in a golden glow and bringing out the rosiness of Elara's cheeks.

"What's wrong?" Hale hadn't moved from his comfy position as he watched me through those intuitive silver eyes.

"Nothing's wrong."

"Rayne, I know that face."

I sighed. "Maybe we planned too much. Two months is a really long time to be away. Elara's going to be one by the time we get back."

"We're coming home the week before her birthday. We talked about this, Rayne. Elara will be in Avalon with my mom and Andrew. We can video conference and see them every day."

"Hale, have you ever tried video conferencing with a toddler?"

"I do it every time I'm away on business."

Hale traveled a lot, so he was used to distance. But I was a homebody. I hadn't been away from Peanut for more than five days since she was born.

He stood, tucking the plush unicorn next to Meep Meep and covering his daughter with a soft blanket.

"You're tense," he said as he gently worked the knots out of my shoulders.

This was how we operated whenever I became neurotic. I'd get worked up and Hale would soothe me. But I didn't want my feelings minimized, so I fidgeted away. "I'm serious, Hale."

"So am I. You have to take it one day at a time. Focus on packing and the rest will all fall into place."

*Maybe for him.* "I'm never going to fit all of this. We're going to too many destinations."

He kissed the side of my neck and a shiver chased down my spine. "You're not going to need half of this. I plan to have you naked most of the time."

"Hale, even if we spend most days in bed, we'll still have to venture out to find food."

"I'll keep you fed." His hand snaked under my T-shirt, palm warm and gentle as he cupped my breast.

I couldn't concentrate when he rolled my nipple like that. "I have to leave some of this stuff behind."

He buried his face in my shoulder, kissing and nipping those sensitive curves and making me twitch. If he made it to my earlobe I was done.

"What about this? Do I need this?" I held up the string bikini Hale's sister had insisted I buy on our last shopping spree.

He pulled the bikini out of my hand and tossed it onto the table. "Come with me."

"But I have to finish packing—"

"You can finish after we're done." He towed me through the penthouse until we were standing in the master bedroom.

"Elara will be awake soon."

"So we better hurry." He stripped out of his shirt and lounge pants.

I backed into the bed. "Hale, I'm still in my PJs."

He caught the front of my faded T-shirt and tugged me forward. "You're full of excuses. Let me distract you."

*Good luck.* I was an incurable over-thinker. And for good reason! Over-thinking helped me prepare for the mul-titude of calamities that befell me regularly. Not everyone was as lucky as Hale.

He crouched and caught me by the back of the knees, flipping me onto the bed. "That's better."

"Hale, I'm not in the right headspace for this. I still have to go through my toi-letries, and pack up the wedding clothes for the cleaner and—*Hello!*"

He yanked down my panties and dove forward, closing his mouth over my clit and pressing his fingers deep. I arched into him, losing my train of thought.

*"There it is!"*

His other hand went to my breasts. This was why the showoff got whatever he wanted in the bedroom. He was a fucking sex god.

"I can't hear you, Rayne. You have to show me you like it or I'll stop."

"Don't you dare stop now!" I fisted his hair, riding his face hard as he teased my clit and drove me over the edge.

He groaned, licking over me as he curled his fingers, dragging out my climax until I was arching off the bed and begging for mercy.

When he finally lifted his face from between my thighs, he smiled with sheer arrogance, dragging his thumb under his lip and then sucking it clean. "Better?"

"I hate you."

He caught my legs, stretched them open, and leaned forward, pressing my knees into the mattress. "That's no way to speak to your husband—especially after he just made you come."

"I told you I had stuff to do." No clue what that stuff was now, but that wasn't the point.

"I can see I still have work to do."

"Hale, no. I have to—"

"Open wide, baby."

"Wait—" He was so quick, pinning my arms over my head and moving up my body. My words cut off as his cock hit the back of my throat. I let out a garbled cry and looked up at him with wide eyes.

"Show me how much you love it when I distract you, then I'll let you go. But be very convincing, Rayne, or I'll keep you here all night."

Another muffled moan. We didn't have all night.

"Eh, eh, eh. Take it like a good girl."

Damn him for using those magic words when I had shit to do. I loosened my jaw and opened my throat—as a good girl does—and he nudged deeper.

"Now, let me see those green eyes." When I looked up at him he groaned. "There's my good little wife." He drew back and thrust slowly, his chiseled body an absolute work of art as he glided in and out effortlessly. "Beautiful, Rayne."

I wasn't sure what it was about seeing to his pleasure that quieted all the noise inside my head. Maybe it was the way he praised me or the absolute command he had over me that set me free. The gentle way he demanded all of my focus relieved me of my worries and control in a way that melted my insides.

"Such a good girl." He cupped the back of my head and my eyes started to tear. "Hold it there."

I did everything he asked. My body was his to command. The longer he took his pleasure the more aroused I became.

Tracing his fingers over my cheek, he wiped away a tear. "Feel better now, baby?"

Drawing back, he fisted his hard length, stroking himself out of my reach so I could answer.

"Yes." Every tense muscle in my body had softened. Even my voice was lower.

"You spoil me, baby."

The truth was, Hale indulged me way more than I spoiled him. Not with material things, though he did love to pamper me with gifts, but with patience and love.

He sat back, stroking his engorged length. "Do you want to stop?"

Feeling pleasantly fragile and protected under his care, I shook my head, always a little shy whenever he tapped into my submissive side.

"No? Did you want more?"

When I nodded, he leaned forward, gently pressing deep again.

Hale never wanted me to be anything other than myself. He never tried to quiet my thoughts or mute my presence. He was interested in every emotion I had and often helped me work through my anxiety in ways I never imagined possible.

The moments when he disrupted my panic and took me away to a place of love and pleasure, a place where I was safe and adored, those were the peaceful moments I lived for.

Despite Hale's intense work schedule and rigid standards, he was always incredibly nurturing with me. He never made me feel insecure or judged. That was how I knew he was my soulmate.

"That's enough." He drew back and repositioned our bodies. "I need to get inside of you."

Pulling me onto his lap, he helped me seat myself. Hale was incredibly well-endowed, so it always took me a moment to adjust.

"That's it, baby. Nice and slow." He held my hips, guiding my body as I lowered.

Our mouths collided in a passionate kiss, then he urged me to ride him faster. I loved those seconds before he finished when his control seemed to slip and something wild flashed in his eyes. All of his usual, carefully crafted, well-bred, pedigree manners disappeared and he became a beast.

Driven by desire and pure, raw ego, he took exactly what he wanted, stretching me to accommodate his pleasure while thrusting hard and fast. "Fuck!"

The greedy way he used my body filled me with a sense of accomplishment

"That's it, baby. Yes." He threw me to my back and caught my wrists, pinning them to the pillows as sweat glistened on his golden skin. "Whose fucking pussy is this?"

"Yours."

"Fucking right it is." He rammed forward, insisting I feel every inch of his hard cock and then we were both coming.

I sometimes wondered if he reflected on the things he said in those fevered moments of passion. But as soon as he finished, his mask of well-bred composure slid back into place.

He kissed me softly. "I love you, Rayne."

"I love you too."

He withdrew, kissing my breasts, my belly, and my clit before leaving the bed. Then the shower turned on. I smirked. Hale hated leaving a mess, but he never minded making one.

I, on the other hand, was of the lazy-bum school of sex. I would loaf around in bed for at least an hour and possibly take a nap.

Or so I thought.

The sound of Elara's voice shifted me right out of my role as newlywed-sex-goddess into mom mode. Maybe it would be nice to get away for a while.

Sliding back into my wrinkled T-shirt, I went to get Peanut.

She smiled when she saw me and held up Meep Meep.

"Did you have a nice nap, Peanut?"

"Meep Meep!" she said, showing me that the stuffed sheep hadn't abandoned her.

I was such a sucker for those pink gums and that toothy grin. "How about we find a snack? Mommy's starved." She climbed into my arms.

The sight of the clothes strewn all over the table returned my anxiety faster than I would have liked. But my head was a little clearer now.

I realized it wasn't so much the wardrobe stressing me out, it was the pressure to make the honeymoon as memorable as possible—sans unforeseeable disasters.

I loved Hale so much, and I wanted him to enjoy this trip. I felt personally responsible for his rest and pleasure over the next two months because, in my goofy head, that would communicate how much I adored and appreciated him.

But they didn't call me Calamity Rayne for nothing, and chances were there would be some hiccups along the way.

# Control Freaks & Calamities

"RAYNE, WHERE'S THE TRAVEL BAG?"

"Which travel bag is that, Hale?" He was driving me crazy.

I had everything sorted in the foyer. Our luggage for the honeymoon was to the left and the boxes getting shipped home on the right. Elara's luggage was waiting to get picked up and transported into the limo taking her, the nanny, and Naomi to New Jersey.

"The black Hermes bag. It had our itinerary in it and the flight information."

"Haven't seen it."

There had been several lists and emails and too many itineraries for me to count since the wedding. Once we said "I do" I decided I was done with all the lists.

Clearly, I was suffering from PTBSD—post-traumatic bride stress disorder. But vacation mode had set in and I was no longer taking on needless obligations or senseless stress.

"I need to check the times for our flights."

"Hale, you've checked the schedules twenty-thousand times. You've rewritten them. You've read them out loud. And you even saved them into your notes on your phone—"

He snapped. "Right!"

*Annnnd, I lost him.*

Hale withdrew his phone to obsess over our unchanged travel schedule some more. "I emailed it to you so you have a copy."

"Great. I was looking for something enthralling to read on the flight."

"I'm just trying to make sure everything goes according to plan."

"I know. And I'm choosing to ignore your anal-retentive, compulsive need to obsess over unchanged details because I love you, and I know this is one of the many ways you love me back. But Hale, if you act like a nitpicky perfectionist once we're on the islands I *will* duct tape your mouth shut." I smiled sweetly. "'Kay?"

He held my stare and shut off his phone. "Point taken."

We were taking the private jet out of JFK International Airport at seven and would be in the air for approximately four hours before landing on the sunny islands of

Turks and Caicos. My stress levels were already plummeting at the mere thought of ocean breezes, weather in the mid-eighties, and passing day after commitment-free day on the powdery white beaches overlooking the turquoise sea. So I wasn't going to let Hale's OCD cramp my chill vibe.

An army of bellmen appeared and Hale directed them with the authority of a military leader. I ignored the chaos and pre-gamed in the kitchen with the butler, who had just made me a delicious margarita.

"I'm going to miss your margaritas, Percy."

"Thank you, madam. But I'm sure they'll have delicious cocktails at your next destination."

"But yours are made with love."

"Thank you, madam. The trick's in the limes and cilantro."

I raised a brow. "Interesting."

"Rayne—" Hale paused in the doorway. "You're drinking?"

I raised a brow. "Are we not supposed to?"

He pocketed his phone and wallet. "The cars will be packed in twenty minutes. It's time to say goodbye to Elara."

My good mood evaporated. This was why I needed alcohol.

Twenty minutes later, Hale was consoling me in the back of the sleek town car as I wept quietly and considered canceling the whole trip.

"She'll be fine, baby. We can check in with them as soon as we land."

I knew he was right, but it felt like I was leaving my heart behind. That regretful sentiment evaporated, however, the moment we hit the islands.

Our villa was an ivory masterpiece, stunningly contrasting against the cerulean blue of the ocean that mirrored the flawless sky. It was our own personal Eden, a literal heaven on earth, and I was on board for a long week full of sin.

We started each day with mind-blowing sex, a few screaming orgasms, then a boozy brunch, and a good morning call to Peanut. We slept off all that hard work on the beach, followed by a soak in the hot spa, and more incredible sex. Each day concluded with a decadent dinner, then night swimming under the stars which inevitably led to—you guessed it—more sex.

I had a feeling Hale was trying to cash in on his wedding gift. I gave him the only thing I knew he really wanted and couldn't buy—consent to knock me up.

Was I ready to have a baby? No, not really. But I hadn't been prepared for half the shit in my life and things were working out okay. Plus, I loved being a mommy to Elara. My life was already full of rattles and diapers, so why not add some more?

After Turks and Caicos, it was off to the Maldives. No private jet on this trip, because that flight was a hell-of-a-long jaunt. Twenty-one freaking hours with only a short layover in between. I experienced every possible emotion on that journey and, honestly, I was shocked Hale hadn't thrown me off the plane at one point. But, man, was it worth it.

Maldives was the perfect idyllic setting for a romantic getaway. The seas were calm, the skies were clear, and the breathtaking coral reefs were just beyond the pristine beaches. This time we were staying in a private little hut right on top of the water. Hale said it was the perfect place for snorkeling and diving.

To be clear, I had never been much of an adventure girl. Nor was I into water sports—or any sports for that matter. Honestly, walking left me winded some days, and I never ran unless something was chasing me. But I was coming to discover Hale was a bit of an adrenaline seeker, so I made arrangements for us to do some underwater exploring.

I was an okay swimmer—meaning I survived by doggy paddle, but Hale had been on the swim team in college. He'd grown up on various coasts. He spent a lot of time at sea on his father's yacht and often sailed with his brother. I should have known I'd be way out of my league.

"Where did you say you rented this equipment?" Hale asked as he examined what I had thought was top-of-the-line snorkeling gear.

"They were advertised on one of the brochures." I'd been slightly persuaded by the cute little cartoon fish in the ad, but now I sensed I might have been swindled. "Does yours smell like fish? Mine smells a little like fish."

Hale sniffed the rubbery material. "Mine smells fine."

I held up my mismatched flippers. "Why?"

"They probably just lost one."

I frowned. Were swimmers returning one fin short? What happened to the other flipper? Was the foot okay? "Are there sharks here?"

"You'll be fine, Rayne. As soon as we're in the water you won't be able to smell anything and you'll be so captivated by the beauty your worries will wash away."

That didn't sound like me. How did one launder a rubber wetsuit?

Hale pulled on his gear and looked like a model in a watersports catalog. I looked like a short, chubby porpoise who would only get cast as the comic relief in a Pixar movie.

"Oh, this is not flattering."

Hale laughed in an aren't-you-cute-and-clueless way. I pursed my lips and scowled. This was not going as I'd imagined.

"The water's warm, Rayne. If you want, skip the wetsuit and go in your suit."

But I wanted to look cool like him. Plus, Hale would be watching me through goggles so I preferred to keep my buoyant parts covered.

"I just need you to zip me up. My string's broken."

Hale had gotten the Mercedes of snorkel gear and I was rocking a 1970's jalopy with rusted parts. I pulled on my mismatched flippers and waddled forward then stilled, looking around.

*What was that?*

I took another few steps along the deck, each one making a squishy fart sound. When I turned back to look at Hale I knew he heard it too.

"My wetsuit's farting!"

"Are you sure it's the suit?"

"That's not me!"

"Of course not. Come on." He walked past me, not a bit of waddle to his steps and no embarrassing sounds coming from his gear.

I thought things would improve underwater, but I was wrong. I couldn't get my mask to seal tightly around my hair, so water continuously leaked into my eyes. I had a limp snorkel which caused me to choke on unwanted drops of water.

"Let me see it," Hale said, stopping his majestic underwater tour to investigate the problem. "Everything looks fine."

But it wasn't fine. "My snorkel has erectile dysfunction."

"We'll switch."

Once I had Hale's mask on there was no more leaking or limp snorkel business, but my mask kept fogging up. Losing vision underwater made me panic, which made the fog worse. Maybe I was claustrophobic.

"Go," I garbled at Hale, who floated majestically about like King Freaking Triton.

I knew he wanted to explore and I was holding him up. Obviously, snorkeling wasn't for me. I found the entire experience rather fatiguing and humiliating.

A school of fish rushed past me and I panicked, bubbles shooting out of my wet suit. I must have made a sound of distress because Hale turned. He pointed the underwater camera in my direction, capturing video. That's when I saw a huge fucking jellyfish and was pretty sure I pissed myself.

*Something to look forward to on the home movies.*

When we returned to land, I was beyond relieved. Hale looked rejuvenated and happy with his gift. How could two people experience one thing so differently?

I waddled back to the dock, my suit farting with every step. I was more than ready to return to the tiki bar on the beach and file snorkeling away as shit I never wanted to do again.

Hale took my hand. "Thanks for arranging that."

"You're welcome." Had he made the arrangements, I probably would have had more fun and a wetsuit that didn't queef. "Did you get some good footage?"

"I did. Take a look." He tipped the screen of the camera, using the shade of the palm trees to block the glare of the sun.

I expected to see coral reefs and exotic fish, but what I saw was a montage of myself, exploring underwater. My hair was wild and waving like a mermaid's and my body looked perfectly fine. I looked…cute.

"You didn't record any of the fish."

"I got footage of all the beauty I wanted to remember."

I looked up at him and smiled. "Hale…"

"What?"

I gave him a shoulder bump, my secret handshake, and code for *I love you.*

He kissed my damp head. "What do you say we get you a cocktail and have a long shower followed by a longer nap."

"I'd say now you're speaking my language."

After Maldives came Seychelles where we stayed in a luxurious treehouse in the lush, tropical forests overlooking the Indian Ocean. There had been a lot of afternoon rain which led to lots of afternoon sex—my kind of adventuring.

Hale had mentioned zip lining but, on account of the weather, I dodged that bullet safely. Thank God.

When we boarded our next flight my

hair had grown twice its usual size. "You're staring."

"So?"

"Look, there's nothing I can do. It's the humidity."

"I think the curls are sexy."

"They're not curls as much as they're inflated frizz."

"Well, I think they're hot. You look like a wild woman. They match the new freckles on the bridge of your nose."

"That's sunburn."

"Still sexy." He stretched out his legs and made himself comfortable as the plane started to move. "Throw you in a tattered rag and we could play Thunderdome."

"Are you having an apocalyptic fantasy right now?"

"Maybe. Or you could wear a little leopard bikini and play my captive, a native souvenir I found in the jungle to see to my pleasure."

Obviously, role-playing was in my near future.

We landed in Bora Bora a full day later. This time I planned better by packing plenty of books. It also helped that I started the flight drunk.

We were back in another stunning over-water bungalow surrounded by a crystal-clear sea. So far, Bora Bora was my favorite. Our luxury hut had a small kitchenette and that inspired me to do something nice for Hale.

I arranged for a few groceries to be delivered and planned to make Hale a home-cooked meal. After weeks away, I thought American comfort food might be appreciated, but I hadn't anticipated how complicated it would be to cook in an under-supplied kitchen.

Breakfast didn't make it to bed as I planned. Instead, Hale awoke in a panic to the shrill squeal of the fire alarm as smoke billowed from the toaster.

"Shit, shit, shit, shit!" I unplugged the machine, unsure what to do with it as the grease from the bacon spattered off the pan and caught fire. "Fire!"

"Get back!" Hale yelled, pushing me aside to move the pan off the flame.

I was about to throw water on it when he stopped me and smothered the blaze with the metal lid, then shut off the burner.

He caught his breath and looked at me. "You okay?"

I coughed and fanned away the smoke. "I'm fine. Did you burn yourself?"

He glanced at the singed hair on his arm. "It's fine. You never throw water on a grease fire, baby."

I knew that, but I'd been in a panic and not thinking. "I just wanted to make you a nice breakfast." All of my hard work was ruined.

He lifted the lid off the pan and plucked up a singed strip of bacon, biting into the black ash. "Delicious."

"Liar. You don't have to eat that."

I tried to take it from him, but he dodged my hand. "I want to eat it. You made it for me."

I rolled my eyes and carried the ruined food to the trash.

"Hey." His arms closed around my shoulders. "Thank you for trying."

While I appreciated his gratitude, I didn't feel I deserved it. First the snorkeling and now this. We would have nothing but memories of calamities to take home with us if I kept trying to do nice things.

"I keep messing up our trip."

"You haven't messed anything up that can't be fixed." He turned me so I was facing him, and then he lifted my chin, forcing me to meet his stare. "You're the only person in the world who does this sort of thoughtful stuff for me, and it is thoughtful. That's what counts. So when I say thank you I mean it, understand?"

I nodded.

"How about you get dressed and we go back to that café we passed yesterday? We'll have a nice breakfast while I arrange to have someone come clean this up, and then we'll spend the day wasting away on the beach. Then we'll check on Elara."

That sounded perfect. And because Hale planned it, it was. No hijinks or hiccups for the rest of the day.

Fifty Shades of Grey fans are falling for
The Surrender Trilogy!

Now, back to your story…

# Things Get Hard

After three weeks of sunny seclusion, I was happy to return to a sense of society, even if it was still a far cry from our normal non-vacation life. The upscale clubs, gourmet restaurants, and designer boutiques of St. Barts brought a welcomed change from our long and lazy beach days.

I wasn't complaining about the lazy days! I could loaf around forever. But Hale was getting antsy.

He was in his glory among all the glamour and sophistication of St. Barts, which allowed him to spoil me when we visited the many affluent boutiques. I didn't need the gifts, but he loved surprising me.

"I just don't understand," I said after he dropped a small fortune on a bag. "Why does anyone need a purse that costs that much? There will be no money left to put in the damn thing."

Hale just laughed. "You know some women appreciate such luxuries."

"I do appreciate it. I just don't get it."

He kissed my head in that affectionate way that said he got a kick out of my logic.

While many women had champagne taste on a beer budget, I was totally content with beer. Hale's wealth overwhelmed me, so I preferred not to think about it. But, as a man who only dated gold-diggers before *moi*, he struggled to accept his fortune wasn't the flex it once was.

After St. Barts, we were off to Fiji to another secluded villa, but this one came with a personal chef—something I think Hale added on last minute after the whole breakfast fiasco.

Fiji was the perfect blend of luxury and adventure with its lush landscapes and impeccable hospitality, but there wasn't much nightlife. After supper, the chef would leave and we were often left to entertain ourselves.

A tropical storm had come through on our last days there. I was cozied up on the indoor hammock reading a naughty little romance I'd picked up at the airport when the music kicked on.

"Paging Mrs. Davenport. Will Mrs. Davenport please come to the bedroom?"

I turned the page amid some hot and heavy book boyfriend fornication. "Mrs. Davenport is reading right now."

Hale appeared in the doorway, antsy from being cooped up all day. "You're still reading that book?"

"It's good."

Hale said something as the hero's pants loosened and he kicked apart the protagonist's feet as she leaned into the wall.

"Earth to Mrs. Davenport." Hale slid his finger down the inside of the spine and lowered the book.

"Hey, I was reading that."

"Hey, your husband needs attention."

I was torn—hunky book boyfriend versus real-life, hunky husband. "I don't know. It's getting really good."

He took the book and tossed it across the room. "I'm better." The hammock rocked violently as Hale climbed beside me.

*"No, no, no, wait!"* My death grip saved me from falling.

"That's better."

I forked my fingers through his soft waves. Sometimes Hale needed a different sort of affection, the kind I don't think he knew existed before me.

He sighed and closed his eyes. "That's nice."

After thirty days together, he seemed to seek out this sort of nurturing more often. I'd hold him and he'd let down his guard. I supposed it was his way of recharging.

Typically, Hale traveled at least once every ten days. We were discovering little things about each other on our honeymoon, but none of those discoveries were bad.

"Do you realize, Hale, that this is the longest consecutive time we spent together since we first met?"

"That wasn't that long ago."

"No, it wasn't." Our honeymoon was going to amount to one-sixth of our total relationship.

The deluge outside pummeled the Koro Sea as the setting sun fought for a place in the sky. The distant mountains created a beautifully moody view.

I kissed his head.

He glanced up at me. "That felt intentional."

"It was."

"What was it for?"

"I was just thinking how far we've come, and how lucky I am to have you." Deep down, I knew we never would have made it this far if not for Hale.

"I'm just as lucky."

He honestly believed that which was another reason I loved him. "Did Rajan go home?"

"About an hour ago. He left you some extra pineapple pie in the fridge."

"Thank you again for getting us a chef." Food was my love language and Hale spoke it very well.

He toyed with the shell buttons of my sundress, sliding them free until my dress parted, enough to fully expose my breasts and belly. His fingers trailed slowly from the lace of my panties to my collar bone and my nipples tightened.

Flattening his palm on my stomach, he asked, "Anything yet?"

It was still too soon, but I was beginning to suspect Hale found a sort of kink in trying to plant his seed in me. I only stopped taking the pill the day after the wedding, but I wasn't sure how long it took to fully get out of my system.

"I'll talk to my doctor when we get home. But it's probably going to take a while, Hale."

"I can be patient while being persistent."

The hammock rocked as he cupped my breast, pulling my puckered nipple to his mouth. I arched beneath his touch, shutting my eyes as he teased the tip with his tongue. The more he ground his body against mine the more the hammock shifted.

"We should go to the bedroom."

"What's wrong with right here?"

The hammock wobbled and I clung to the sides. "I'm afraid we're going to flip. I can't relax."

"I won't let you flip." He plumped my

breasts and went back to what he was doing.

"*Ah!* Did you just bite me?"

He gave me a devilish grin. "Did it hurt?"

I frowned. It was more shocking than anything else. "A little."

"Did you like it?"

My cheeks heated. "A little."

"Interesting." He nipped me again.

"*Hale!*"

"I like your nipples dark and swollen." He brushed his lips softly over the hard tips. "Let me make you come this way."

I doubted that was possible. "You can try."

"Is that a challenge?"

I leaned back and stretched open my arms. "I'm all yours."

"Good girl." He kissed one nipple. "Such a good little wife." Then he kissed the other. "So eager to please." When his mouth closed over the tip he wasn't messing around.

My back bowed and I moaned at the intense shock, but then something happened. The harder he sucked the better it felt. My insides tightened and my sex pulsed.

He released my swollen flesh with a pop. "Look at that."

I glanced down, startled by how dark and turgid he'd made the tip. Then he pinched it.

*"Ah!"*

"So fucking sexy." He grinned and latched on to the other one, sucking equally as hard.

When I squirmed, he held me tight, forcing me to come to peace with the slight sting. Just like before, the sharp tease of pain shifted into something dark and delicious before it truly hurt.

When he pulled away I angled my body toward him, silently seeking more and not at all shocked that Hale could show me something new and have me begging for it in no time at all.

"You like it?"

I bit my lip and nodded. Tomorrow would likely be a different story, but right now it felt incredible.

He plumped my breasts and went to town. The son of a bitch was right. The longer he sucked and pinched the more erotic it felt. Soon enough, I was enjoying a delicate little orgasm from nothing but nipple play.

"Can we please go to the bedroom now?" I needed him inside of me.

"Not a chance. Stay put." The hammock swung as he stood and stripped off his clothes. Then he repositioned me so I was sitting on the hammock like a swing, facing him. When he stripped away my dress, he paused to admire my nipples. "Look how red and engorged they are. Do they hurt?"

He grazed the tips with a gentle finger and I sucked in a sharp breath. "They're sensitive."

"Good. Lean back." The moment I did he stripped away my panties. "These are very wet, Mrs. Davenport."

My skin burned. "Well, what do you expect, Mr. Davenport?"

"How about a thank you?"

I rolled my eyes. "Thank you for

breaking my nipples and making me come."

He stepped forward, fisting his hand in my hair and angling my face for a kiss, only to tease me with his mouth and make me want him all the more.

"I'd never break you." He finally kissed me softly. "But I am going to fuck you—hard. Ready?"

"Yeh—" Before I had the word out, he caught my knees and pulled me to the edge of the hammock. Gripping my ankles, he opened my body in a wide V and thrust deep.

I gripped the canvas and gasped. The hammock created a sense of weightless ease that let him slide my body however he wanted. Over and over, he pulled me into him, slamming his cock deep and hard.

"I wish you could see how fucking beautiful you look right now. Mine. Spread open as I slide my cock in and out of your wet pussy. I'm going to fuck you so hard you'll feel me inside of you for days. And you're going to let me, aren't you?"

"Yes," I gasped.

"That's my good girl."

He released my legs, letting them drape over his muscled arms as he controlled the hammock, sliding me into him and pushing me back. Over and over he seated himself to the hilt. Pelvis to pelvis. Every time I slammed down on him he brought me closer to the euphoric madness only he could create.

"Pinch your nipples, Rayne. Hold them tight and don't let go."

I was lost, swinging into him like a pleasure toy he could fuck as hard and freely as he desired. He grunted, telling me how much he loved me. Loved fucking me. Loved watching me. Loved tasting me. Loved possessing me the way no other man ever would. Then I was screaming and coming all over his dick.

He went deeper and was able to fuck me harder the more I surrendered. By the time he finished, I was worthless. Far too tired to move to the bedroom, so we both curled up on the hammock and slept there, listening to the rain and watching the moon reflect on the water through the clouds.

As expected, my tits were killing me the next day. The slightest movement had me gasping in exquisite pain and re-membering how good he'd made me feel the night before.

When we buckled in for another long flight, I said, "I think we need to invest in a hammock when we get home."

"Say less." He was already pulling out his phone and placing the order. "Done."

# Aloha!

We arrived in Italy the following morning and took a boat into the harbor on the Amalfi Coast. Our villa overlooked the Mediterranean Sea and provided a breathtaking view of the brightly colored villages. But I was most excited about the food.

Of course Hale spoke flawless Italian, so he was a great tour guide. He couldn't remember how many times he'd visited, but he guessed he'd been to Italy at least thirty times. The man seriously got around.

The first night we feasted on *spaghetti alle vongole*, and the next night it was *scialatielli ai frutti di mare*. I tried *tortellini alla caravella* and *bistecca alla fiorentina*. But my absolute favorite was the *ravioli di ricotta e limone*.

Five days and my clothes were snugger than ever, but I had absolutely no regrets. "I think we should stay here."

Hale laughed. "I knew you'd love Italy. And this is only the Amalfi Coast. Wait until we come back and visit Tuscany. You'll love the North. It's a much more leisurely pace up there.

The man did know me well. I lived for the slow stuff. "Is there any of the *zeppole* left?"

He tossed me a small bag filled with the sugary fried dough. I opened it up and frowned. "What's this? What's *gravidanza?*"

"Don't eat it." He teased, taking the package out of my hand and opening the box. "You pee on it. It's a test."

"Hale." I rolled my eyes. "I told you, it's too soon."

"It's been five and a half weeks, Rayne. And we've had sex nearly every day without interruption."

"But these things take—oh shit." I did quick-period math. We left New York on April eleventh and I hadn't had my period since two weeks before the wedding.

It had been a lot longer than five weeks.

"Give me the test."

He handed the applicator over and followed me into the bathroom.

I looked up at him expectantly. "Are you waiting for something?"

"Does this bother you?"

I did very little things gracefully. The vision of me aiming my pee at a tiny stick might be hard to shake. "Yes. A little privacy please."

"As you wish." He shut the door.

I was not good at directing my stream and very grateful I hadn't let him stick around to watch. After washing my hands I brought the stick out to the kitchen where Hale waited at the table.

Together, we stared at it.

"What are the rules?" I asked. "Is it still plus and minus in Italy?"

"Have you taken a lot of pregnancy tests before?"

"No, but I watch television. I know how these things work. In America at least."

He read the tiny words. "Two lines if it's positive, one line for negative."

I chewed on my thumb nail as the first line appeared. "How long does it take?"

"We should know in a few minutes."

"And where did you say the *zeppole* was?"

He slid another paper bag in front of me. This one actually filled with sugary dough. I took a large bite and chewed anxiously.

It had to be done by now.

"It's negative," he said, snatching it off the table and tossing it in the trash.

"Are you mad?"

"Not mad, just disappointed."

"Hale, we just started trying. You have to be patient."

"I am being patient." I picked up his iPad and headed into the den.

I followed. "What are you doing?"

"Just checking on some work things."

He was in a mood I didn't feel like navigating. "Paging Mr. Davenport…" I teased, but he only half smiled. "Hey." I stole his tablet. "This isn't a simple thing and you're making it feel like a failure when it's not."

He sighed. "You're right. I'm sorry."

I climbed onto his lap and wreathed my arms around his shoulders. "It'll happen when it's meant to happen."

He pressed his forehead to mine and grinned, his hand sliding to my belly. "I can't wait to see you pregnant, to see what our child will look like."

I smiled at the sweet thought. "Will she have green or grey eyes?"

"I hope she looks just like you."

"And if it's a boy?"

"Then I hope he has your sense of humor."

"And your business sense—for a boy or a girl," I added.

He stroked my cheek, tucking my hair behind my ear as he pulled me in for a slow kiss. "Let's try again," he whispered, already stripping away my clothes.

Conscious of the open windows and the fact that we were in a very small village with busy sidewalks and tourists passing, I kept my body turned so only Hale could see my bare chest. He kissed my shoulders and breasts.

"Loosen my pants."

I reached between us and lifted as he pushed my dress up to my hips. Sliding my panties aside, I lowered onto his hard length and we both moaned.

"Put a baby in me, Hale."

His fist tangled in my hair as he kissed me hard. My body rocked as I rode him, our breathy moans accompanied by the Italian conversations drifting by. He guided my hips, thrusting upward, as he smothered his face in my chest.

"Fuck. Keep going."

The muscles in my legs started to scream, but it felt too good to stop. My hand snaked between us, and I rubbed my clit. He was close and I wanted to finish with him.

I started to panic at my inability to bring myself to climax. "Can you make me come?"

He pulled me forward and I lunged closer, confused when my chin rested on his shoulder. "Stay still for a second."

I stilled and my eyes widened when his finger pushed into my ass. "Hale…"

"Shh… You're okay."

He was deep, filling me from both angles. "I don't know what to do."

"Let your body sink onto me and relax. I've got you."

Leaning into him, I lowered until his cock fully penetrated me. That's when his finger started to move.

I sucked in a breath. Stretched and unsure, I held onto his shoulders and let him lead. Sensations zipped over my nerves and I gasped.

He teased the thin wall separating his stroking finger from his engorged cock. "That's a good wife. Stay still and let your husband take care of you."

I was shocked by how much he was making me feel. I wasn't even riding him anymore, but my sex had started to clench and my clit was pulsing.

"Now, touch yourself, baby."

I reached between us and started to rub, gasping when the first shiver of an orgasm stole through me. "Oh, my God."

"Keep going," he said, pumping his finger in and out. "You're almost there. I can feel you tightening around me."

"Ah…" My head fell back as a wash of pleasure rained over me. I trembled and Hale held me close, riding the storm with me until we were both panting and replete.

"Beautiful."

I would always favor Italy a little more than all the other places we visited because that was where Hale made the impossible possible. He might have destroyed my modesty that day, fucking me in broad daylight while villagers walked by the open windows—some had undoubtedly looked in. But what they saw was a woman in command of her own pleasure. A woman in love with an incredible man. A woman set free.

I could have stayed in Italy forever, but we had two more stops to make. Next was Santorini, Greece, which I was relieved to learn was only a short three-hour flight away from the Amalfi Coast.

Santorini was very similar to the Amalfi Coast with its busy streets and heavy tourist attractions, but the atmosphere was slightly different in that it lacked the brightly colored architecture of Amalfi.

Homes stacked along the coast like a pile of salt building from the briny sea. Each one uniquely carved of the same white stone. The crisp, bleached landscape was stunning at sunset when the sky seemed to reflect off the crystal clear waters and illuminate the buildings in shades of pink and gold.

I hadn't felt great in Greece. It might have been all the walking, or perhaps it was the non-stop seafood we'd eaten, or maybe the stubborn jackass I rode on the way in. *Not Hale, but the actual donkey he stuck me on to get to the villa.*

"I'm sorry you didn't get to enjoy Greece as much as all our other stops," Hale said toward the end of our stay.

I'd been exhausted and fighting a stomach bug. "I'm sure we'll come back."

"I promise we will."

I smiled up at him adoringly, knowing he'd keep his word.

By the time our stay ended, I was ready to go home. I missed American food and my creature comforts. I missed drive-throughs, central air, and ice in my drinks. But most of all, I missed Elara.

The last time we video chatted with her she looked enormous. She was saying new words and toddling around like a pro. And we were missing it.

I had a hunch Hale was also homesick for his daughter, but he seemed determined to make sure we enjoyed every last minute of our trip. We had one more stop in Maui and then it was back to Key West where I planned to stay for a long time.

When we landed in Hawaii I suddenly recalled a lot from my high school geography class. Namely, how the island was famous for its volcanos.

Hale thought this was a silly concern, but if anyone was going to suffer a brutal death in liquid-hot volcanic magma, it was probably me. My abnormally lucky husband would find the one dry spot in an eruption and outlive us all.

Knowing there was only one week left of our honeymoon I made the most of it.

We spent the first day on the beach, but after that, it was all about Hale.

I booked us a tour through the rainforest, which was incredible. Then we took surfing lessons, which was hilarious. Hale picked the skill up in an instant. Me, not so much.

For our last night, I booked us a reservation at a restaurant known for its eccentric dining experience and unique menu. It was one of those fancy places where the chef picks the menu for guests and they only serve so many people a night. Very exclusive. Very Hale.

"Where did you find this place?" he asked as we entered through a grotto covered by a pergola wrapped in a year's worth of flowers and twisting vines.

"The surfing instructor's girlfriend told me about it when you were out riding the waves."

They had our table ready when we arrived. What I didn't expect was to be sitting with other people, but apparently, every night was broadcast live on the restaurant's YouTube channel. Had I known that, I would have watched a few episodes first.

We introduced ourselves to the two other couples dining with us. One woman appeared drunk and the other looked bored. The men, however, were sociable and eager to chat.

"Rayne, is it?"

I nodded and the man held out a large hand.

"Name's Bob. This is Judy. We're from Oklahoma. Where are you two from?"

"We live in Key West." I didn't see the need to explain that Hale had multiple houses all over the country.

"Key West is great. We vacation there with friends every fall. We call our little club the Upside-Down-Pineapples."

"Oh, that's…nice," I said, unsure if that was important information for me to have.

"Why the pineapples?" Hale asked.

"When you know, you know," Bob said, shooting me an exaggerated wink.

I guess I didn't know. Still, I didn't want to appear unfriendly so I said, "I love pineapples! They're one of my favorite snacks."

Bob grinned. "I bet you got a real sweet tooth, don't you, Rayne?"

"You know it."

I glanced at Judy, who was face-planting in her cocktail. She didn't look interested in anything her husband was saying so I looked at the other couple. "And your names?"

"This is Laura and I'm Norbert."

I snapped my mouth shut. Did he say his name was Norbert? I could not be around people with silly names and Norbert was a name of a chubby headliner in a comic strip.

This time Hale didn't bail me out. He knew a name like that would kill me, and no matter how composed he appeared I sensed him laughing at me on the inside. *Bastard.* I'd show him that I could hold a conversation like a sophisticated adult.

"So…*Norbert*—" I swallowed back a laugh. "What do you do for a living?"

"I'm a minister of merriment."

*Uh-oh.* I ignored the giggles building in my stomach. "And what is that, exactly?"

Norbert grinned. "Well, I own my own business, so technically I'm the Jester-in-Chief or Head Honcho of Hilarity. *Hey-oh!*" He laughed, elbowing his wife who looked like she could think of a million places she'd rather be.

I cocked my head, still a little confused about his business and feeling like I missed the punchline of his joke.

Laura rolled her eyes, but not in a playful way. "He's a clown."

I stilled. "A… c—clown, did you say?" As a lifelong sufferer of coulrophobia, this was no laughing matter.

"Want to see a trick?"

"Oh, God, no, please!" I drew back in my seat and clung to Hale.

That was enough about Norbert. Turning back to the pineapple winker, I smiled. "Where'd you get that drink, Judy?"

"The waitress."

*I'd sure like to meet her.*

"Tonight's gonna be a hoot," Norbert announced, but I couldn't bring myself to look at him. What if he was suddenly wearing a red nose?

When the waitress finally returned, I ordered a margarita, but that was a no-go. The chef even picked the cocktails and tonight we were all having pink squirrels—whatever the hell that was.

"And what exactly is this?" I stirred the milky pink drink and sniffed, finding the scent nutty with a trace of choco-late-covered cherries. "Hale, smell this?"

He leaned over and sniffed the glass then cleared his throat. "That's…interesting."

I begrudgingly sipped the concoction and gagged. "It wants to be pink milk, but it's not."

The centerpieces were cleared to make room for the main course, which we still hadn't been told about. Remington once told me it was rude to ask too many questions when dealing with eccentric chefs. So I trusted the experience.

But when the main course arrived, my easy going attitude disappeared. "Um…" I leaned close to Hale. "That pig's staring at me."

"Which one?"

What did he mean, which one? "The one with the apple in its mouth." Who knew I had hard limits with food?

When I looked to see if anyone else was disturbed by the sight Pineapple Bob winked at me. What the hell was this guy's deal?

Hale tossed his linen napkin over the pig's head. "He winks at you one more time, and I'm going to do to him what they did to Wilber."

I scrunched my nose. *Ew.* "He's old, Hale," I whispered, trying to be discreet.

"That's irrelevant. You're my wife and he's been eye-fucking you since we sat down."

I cleared my throat, staring down at my empty plate and disgusting drink. Maybe we should leave.

"What's got you acting so shy all of a sudden?" Bob asked and Hale snapped.

"That's it!"

"Whoa." Bob held up his hands. "Easy now."

"Wink at my wife again and I'll—"

"I thought you were okay with it."

"Why the hell would I be okay with another man flirting with my wife?"

"Guess you two don't swing that way."

What the… *Oh!* I placed a calming hand on Hale's leg. "Honey, I think an upside-down pineapple is code for being a swinger."

"Smart little cookie you got there, Hale."

He growled. "Hit on her again and I'll show you just how hard I swing, understand?"

"Loud and clear."

This was a nightmare.

"Maybe we should leave," I whispered.

Hale glanced at me, all of his frustration vanishing. "No. You planned a nice dinner and I plan to enjoy it." He squeezed my hand. "Do you want some—"

"No." My stomach lurched.

Unfortunately, things only got worse. The next course was fried frog legs. And for dessert, we had a choice, spaghetti ice cream or chocolate-covered pickles. I chose neither, as did Hale.

The moment we left the restaurant he doubled over in laughter.

"It's not funny!"

"Oh, Rayne, it's pretty fucking funny!" He wiped his eyes. "Your expression was priceless when they brought out that pig! And then the frog legs." He laughed harder than I ever saw him laugh.

"I was trying to do something nice for you!"

"This was unforgettable!"

"This was a disaster, Hale! You just threw down four hundred dollars for an evening with clowns and swingers, and all I had was one sip of a shitty cocktail."

"Thank you so much for bringing me here. I'm never going to forget this!"

I left him to his hysteria and stomped off to the rental car, closing myself inside so I could sulk. When Hale finally joined me, he was composed. Until he wasn't.

Losing the battle against the apparent hilarity, he dropped his head onto the steering wheel and cracked up some more, his shoulders bouncing as he howled.

"Jerk," I said, whacking him with my tiny purse.

"Why am I a jerk?" He wiped the tears from his eyes.

"Because you're laughing at me."

"Baby, no. I'm not laughing at you. I'm laughing at us."

"But it's not funny! I had eight weeks and every time I tried to do something nice for you it blew up in my face. First the farting scuba gear, then the kitchen fire. And now this!"

He threw his head back and barked out another laugh. "I forgot about the farting wet suit!"

"Hale!"

"Baby, don't you see? In eight weeks we didn't have one single fight. We feasted, and drank, and explored, and played. We fucked and had two whole months of fun. I laughed harder than I've ever laughed before. Why? Because life's so much better with you."

Well, when he put it that way it didn't sound too bad. "Really? I did that for you?"

"Yes, you!" He pulled me close and kissed me. "You make me happier than I believed possible, Rayne. I love you."

"I love you too."

"And think of the memories we get to take with us. I never want to forget a single silly thing you do." He tucked my hair behind my ear. "Don't you see, baby? You did give me something—something priceless."

I pressed my forehead to his. "How do you do that?"

"Do what?"

"Put a positive spin on a bad situation."

"Bad? Why? Because dinner was weird? Who cares? Look around, Rayne. We're in Hawaii. We've been to Fiji, Bora Bora, Italy, and Greece. Our hut could have burnt down. My favorite part about this whole trip was spending it with you. That's all that matters."

He was right. Richer or poorer, through sickness and health, our love was what mattered most.

I lowered my head and chuckled, laughing at how ridiculous some of our adventures had been. "I nearly died when Norbert said he was a clown."

"A Minister of Merriment!" Hale barked.

"The Head Honcho-of-Hilarity!" I laughed with him, finally seeing the humor of it all.

We fell to pieces, cracking up until our stomachs cramped. It was the perfect end to a perfect vacation. I never thought about the actual word honey-moon before, but I got it now. I was over the moon for this man. And he was over the moon for me.

## THE END

*No fish, clowns, pigs, or swingers were harmed in the making of this novella.*
*WANT MORE CALAMITY?*

*CLICK HERE to pre-order Calamity Rayne Knocked Up!*

*"Now," he whispered, his nose nuzzling that sensitive spot below my ear. "Let's try this again."*

*His eyes narrowed, and he got back to work. I did some period math in my head to calculate how long I'd have to wait until the next fertile day of my cycle.*

*"That's it." He snapped, flipping me to my stomach. "I tried being patient with you, Rayne." The drawer opened, and he tossed something on the bed.*

*Lube? "Hold on!"*

*CLICK HERE* to pre-order *Calamity Rayne Knocked Up!*

Want more sexy billionaires from Lydia Michaels?
Don't miss Mr. Stone is BLIND
**Turn the page for a FREE sample…**

Or if you want to skip right to the good stuff, download the whole book by clicking HERE!

# Blind



"Are you comfortable?"

She nodded in the darkness, unsure if the tumultuous excitement brimming inside reached the realm of comfortable, but this was exactly where she wanted to be—the point she'd waited so long to reach.

This was it, the moment Scarlet Farrow had been anticipating for three grueling months. In the darkness of her mind, colors swirled, forming a tapestry of imagined characteristics for this mysterious man. He was her every hidden fantasy come to life.

*Mr. Stone.*

Warmth bloomed low in her belly as she breathed in his mysterious presence, savoring every memorized detail of the stranger who'd somehow heightened her passions and laid her bare —all prior to setting eyes on him. There was no way to define the array of emotion he provoked in her.

Her throat went dry as his fingertip ghosted over her larynx, barely touching, utterly titillating. Only *he* could provoke such a reaction, simply whisper one question and call her entire being into compliance.

The cool air of the room chilled her exposed shoulders, yet her skin burned for every long awaited caress. There was something about blindness that awakened the senses, goaded courage, and turned vulnerability into raw hunger. Need.

She had no idea what the room looked like, how it was dressed or furnished. According to her other senses, she imagined it massive, with high reaching ceilings and walls somewhat vacant.

From the beginning he'd claimed to know what she required, but after years of disappointing blind dates and lackluster sex, Scarlet was initially skeptical. She'd been wrong. He knew what she needed, and through many lessons in patience and honesty, a side of her she never anticipated surfaced for him. Every fleeting moment in the company of Mr. Stone was worth the seemingly endless waiting—he was *that* impressive.

Burgeoning trust turned to pure, carnal need. It was the liaison of a lifetime, a masterpiece of emotions tied into this, their last moment of blindness, when all would finally be unveiled.

She'd done everything he'd asked, followed every meticulous command down to the last detail. Unsure of his physique or even the expression he wore, her attraction had nothing to do with his body or the smoldering way his gaze scrutinized her nakedness. Perhaps his eyes didn't smolder at all, but his words, his tone, always spoke of an intensity that went beyond the physical and sent her insides ablaze.

She craved his drugging affection with every aching piece of her soul.

He aroused her, not physically, but with intellect, challenging her, pressing her, and unraveling her until the physical need rivaled the screaming desire for his total possession. Simply put, he *saw* her. Exposed. Vulnerable. Raw.

"I need you present, Ms. Farrow."

Understanding the magnitude of this moment, she reassured him every part of her being was invested in the now. "I'm here, Mr. Stone. Always here."

Her body shivered, as her spine lengthened, pulling her shoulders back as her shins pressed into the cool floor. He'd stripped her of more than her clothing. Stripped away her veils, stripped away her ego, stripped away her choice, and all at her eager consent.

The soft click of his shoes over exposed floor halted her breath, reminding her that he was clothed, holding the upper hand to her vulnerable nudity. The echoes, found only in drafty openness of this place, were now familiar.

Never in her life had she placed so much trust in another, let alone in an absolute stranger. He was an unexpected risk, a secret others wouldn't understand. Coming here was a brave decision and she had no regrets. Never before had she been so proud of her courage.

"You're pleased." It wasn't a question, but a confident observation.

He saw through her facades, unveiled the parts of her the rest of the world never bothered to see. He exposed her soul, her bare need, and her darkest desires.

It would be impossible to lie to him. Lips twitching with a hidden smile, she confessed, "I am."

"And so you should be. It's been quite a journey."

Breath dragged into her lungs with each ragged inhalation as if filling her up like a balloon that would soon pop. Everything they'd built together rested in this final moment of truth.

Eagerness to rush forward had her trembling. His finger caressed the soft pad of her lower lip and the sharp rush of familiar excitement came with the touch of his flesh to hers, rocking her off balance.

"Be still."

Her chin quivered as the backs of his soft nails traveled over her jaw, behind her ear, and down her throat. His touch was always so tender, almost hesitant and slightly reverent. It was revealing in a way, because he embodied confidence, control, and patience, yet his gentle touch sometimes spoke of diffidence.

Those refined caresses resembled unspoken secrets, so worshipful and vulnerable in a way she couldn't comprehend. Whoever he was outside of this room, beyond his power, she believed he was innately kind.

"It isn't fair for a woman to hold such beauty," he whispered.

His thumb coasted over the soft curve of her throat, tripping slowly over each ridge of her larynx, teasing the slight curve of her collarbone. Her nipples tightened painfully as the anticipation breathed like fire in her pulsing veins. Her nerves never rested in his presence.

What he so carefully built between them went beyond mere sexual titillation. It was deep, plunging far past the shallow reality most couples shared. Mr. Stone was a man of few words so she savored every confession, every clue, every query, each one a fragment of the masterpiece of this mysterious man.

"When I read your letter, I knew there was something special about you, Ms. Farrow. While there was courage in your words, I sensed the absolute desperation of your plea. True, you did not ask to be found—only to be heard—but I found you all the same. Genuine courage is not borne of fear. True courage takes action, despite the fear. You, my lady, feared what?"

So much. She feared leaving this world incapable of describing what it felt like to be loved. He was right. She hadn't written the letter because she was brave. She'd written it because she was scared, terrified the life she'd led was all there would ever be.

"I feared always being alone."

"Correct. Yet, you've given months to a complete stranger, trusting me to show you something that changes nothing of your predicament outside of these walls. Why?"

The burn of truth wasn't as severe as it once had been. At this point, she was so exposed there was hardly anything left to hide. "I wanted to know what it felt like to be adored, cared for, placed at the top of someone's priority list, Mr. Stone. You said you could give me that experience."

"Do you feel you've achieved your goal, Ms. Farrow? Have you felt those very things?"

Her heart raced. "Yes."

"And do you have any regrets, Ms. Farrow?"

He never bullied her or even pressured her. He merely offered, and while the entire turn of their correspondence had taken her off guard, it was her decision to go to him—on his terms and her trust.

The moment she agreed, life as she knew it was forever changed. Every instruction, every stipulation, disentangled another part of her. Desire bloomed into reckless curiosity as hidden secrets were slowly revealed.

"I have no regrets."

WANT TO KEEP READING? Click HERE!

Hard Fix

Intentional Risk

**JASPER FALLS**

Wake My Heart *

The Best Man

Love Me Nots

Pining For You

My Funny Valentine

Side Squeeze

**CALAMITY RAYNE**

Calamity Rayne  Gets a Life *

Calamity Rayne Back Again

Calamity Rayne Gets Hitched

BONUS: Calamity Rayne Veiled & Railed

Calamity Rayne Over the Moon

Calamity Rayne Knocked Up

**THE SURRENDER TRILOGY**

Falling In

BreakingOut

Coming Home

**Ruthless Billionaires**

One Billion Secrets *

Two Billion Enemies

**MASTERMIND**

Blind

Untied

**NEW CASTLE**

First Comes Love *

If I Fall

Shattered Vows

**ADDICTED TO YOU**

Crush *

Bang

Throb

## THE ORDER OF VAMPIRES

Original Sin *

Dark Exodus

Prodigal Son

Immortal Bastard

Primal Kill

Blood Moon

## STAND ALONES

La Vie en Rose

Simple Man

Sugar

Breaking Perfect

Hurt

Protege

# About the Author

To receive Lydia's Newsletter and 7 FREE Books, click HERE !

Free Books Here!

Lydia Michaels is the bestselling and award-winning author of more than forty novels. She writes heart-clenching, unpredictable romance with dark elements and high heat. Her work is character-driven and bursting with broken heroes and badass females. With a sweet spot for overbearing, territorial types, her deeply emotional books are spicy, emotionally satisfying, and guaranteed to leave readers with many book hangovers.

Lydia is the consecutive winner of the *2018 & 2019 Author of the Year Award* from *Happenings Media* and the recipient of the *2014 Best Author Award* from the Courier Times. She has been featured by *USA Today*, *Romantic Times Magazine*, the *Women in Publishing Summit*, and more.

Michaels started her author career in 2007, becoming a recognized presence and advocate within the publishing industry. She is the **CEO** of **LMC** Consulting, a certified author coach specializing in character and plot development, and the founder of the *East Coast Author Convention*, the *Behind the Keys*

*Author Retreat*, and <u>www.LydiaMichaels-Books.com</u>.

She is happily married to her childhood sweetheart. Her favorite things include cooking Italian cuisine, hosting extravagant dinner parties, sipping espresso martinis, listening to her husband play piano, and escaping to her coastal home on the Jersey Shore. She's an LGBTQ ally, a BLM supporter, a firm believer that the patriarchy must end (women's rights are human rights), and an advocate for pediatric cancer research.

LYDIA

Follow Lydia Michaels on social media!
Facebook | Instagram | TikTok

# Thank you for your review!

Reviews help authors so much!
If you left a review for this
book, I greatly appreciate it!
Thank you,
Lydia

## Click here to leave your review!

www.ingramcontent.com/pod-product-compliance
Lightning Source LLC
Chambersburg PA
CBHW021720190726
48289CB00008B/2612